Blue's
⊙ Read-Together ⊙
Storybook

Simon Spotlight/Nick Jr.

New York   London   Toronto   Sydney   Singapore

Based on the TV series *Blue's Clues*® created by Traci Paige Johnson,
Todd Kessler, and Angela C. Santomero as seen on Nick Jr.®
On *Blue's Clues*, Steve is played by Steven Burns.

SIMON SPOTLIGHT
An imprint of Simon & Schuster Children's Publishing Division
1230 Avenue of the Americas, New York, New York 10020
Blue Is My Name and *Magenta and Me*
© 2000 Viacom International Inc. All rights reserved.
My Favorite Letters, *Meet My Family*, and *My Pet Turtle*
© 2001 Viacom International Inc. All rights reserved.
NICKELODEON, NICK JR., *Blue's Clues*, and all related titles, logos,
and characters are trademarks of Viacom International Inc.
All rights reserved, including the right of reproduction
in whole or in part in any form.
READY-TO-READ, SIMON SPOTLIGHT, and colophon are registered
trademarks of Simon & Schuster.
Manufactured in the United States of America
First Edition
2 4 6 8 10 9 7 5 3 1
ISBN 0-689-85144-8
These titles were previously published
individually by Simon Spotlight.

Contents

Blue Is My Name

by Angela C. Santomero
illustrated by Karen Craig

Hi, it's me,  !
BLUE

I'm so 😊 to see you.
HAPPY

is my name.
Do you know why?

BLUE

11

Because  is the
color of the **BLUE** .

SKY

12

13

BLUE is the color of my favorite **BIRD** in a **TREE**. The bird's **BLUE** like me, can you see?

14

is the color of the  in my .

BLUE

WATER

BATHTUB

17

is the color

of my   .

Rub! Rub! Rub!

19

20

Blue is the 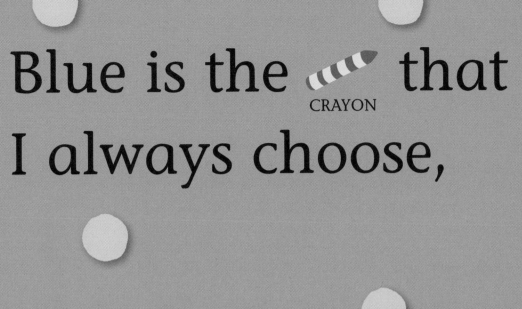 that
I always choose,

when I write the number 2 2 2 .
TWO

is also the color of my  and  !

BLUE

RAINHAT

SHOES

23

is found in my

BLUE

favorite PANCAKES **.**

24

Just like the ones 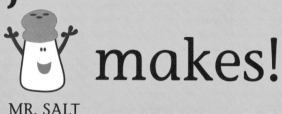 makes!

MR. SALT

Shake! Shake! Shake!

26

is my name.
BLUE
I'm proud, don't
you see...

because  is
BLUE
the color of me!

30

Magenta and Me

by Deborah Reber
illustrated by Don Bishop

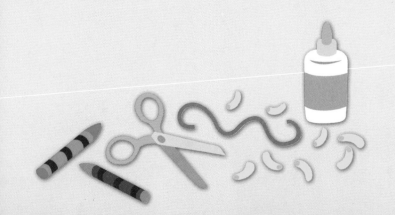

Hi, it's me, ! BLUE
And this is my best
friend, !
MAGENTA

has and big ears just like me!

34

But she's  and
I'm , so we're
different, you see?

 **MAGENTA** **and I met on our first day of** **SCHOOL** **.**

36

We were both a little shy, but  SCHOOL was so cool!

Now we see each other at  almost every day.

SCHOOL

We read , paint

BOOKS

, and take time

PICTURES

to play!

39

When  reads

MISS MARIGOLD

BOOKS

, we sit together

on the reading .

RUG

And when it's time to say good-bye, we give each other a 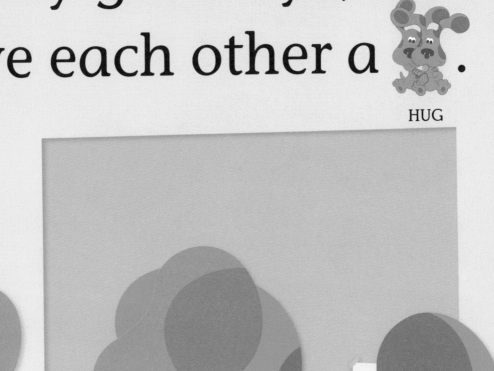.

HUG

Some days  comes

MAGENTA

over to play after 🏫.

SCHOOL

42

Then we play in the  or swim in my .

SANDTABLE

POOL

Other times we
try to find  BIRDS
in the .
TREES

44

Then we make
a  of the
LIST   BIRDS
we see.

If it's  we play
RAINING
different games in
my .

ROOM

46

Like marching parade with my
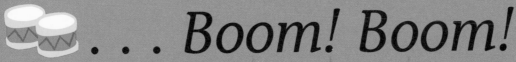 . . . *Boom! Boom!*
Boom!

DRUMS

is so silly, she's always making me things.

She made me this ⬭ out of 🍝 and 〰.

BRACELET   NOODLES   STRING

She also drew this  that I hung on my wall.

MAGENTA knew that my
favorite season
was fall.

Look, I'm making a  for today.

PRESENT

MAGENTA

It's a big "M" for that I made out

MAGENTA

of .

CLAY

And here is my 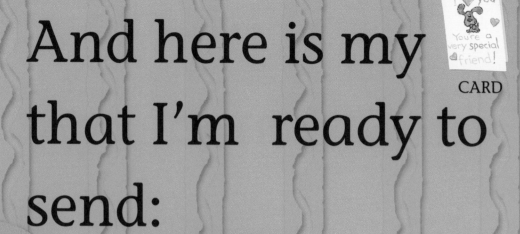 CARD
that I'm ready to
send:

54

My Favorite Letters

by Deborah Reber
illustrated by Karen Craig

Hi, I am ! I just
learned to spell my
name at .

BLUE

SCHOOL

57

B-L-U-E! They are my **4** favorite
<small>FOUR</small>
letters in the whole alphabet!

Look, I wrote my name in the  SAND TABLE with a STICK. Can you see? Even the CLOUDS are spelling my name!

61

The  in the
FLOWERS

 can spell my
GARDEN

name, too.
What great letters!
And they start so
many great words.

B begins my name, and it begins lots of words in this picture I made. It is called "'s in

BLUE   BUBBLES

the ."

BATHTUB

64

Here is the  that  got me for my birthday!

BOOK

BABY BEAR

MR. SALT and MRS. PEPPER are baking

BANANA BREAD for Steve.

Baking BANANA BREAD. All of those words start with B!

And look!

Here is something that starts with L: 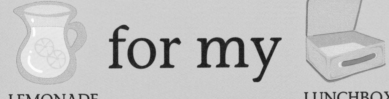 for my  to take with me to !

LEMONADE

LUNCHBOX

SCHOOL

Here is a  LETTER from

MAGENTA that makes me

laugh out loud!

 LETTER, laugh, and

loud all start with

L too!

What about U? I like that letter, too. It is the first letter of 🌂.

UMBRELLA

And U is the first letter of . Do you like U? Me too!

UNDERWEAR

And then there is E.
E is the first letter
for 👂👂 , elbows,
EARS
and 👀 !
EYES
I can build an E
with ice cream ≡
STICKS
and 🧴 .
GLUE

75

Or, I can paint the  on my .

EARTH

EASEL

76

E is the first letter of .They go inside

ENVELOPES

. Look!  has

MAILBOX   MAILBOX

a  for me!

LETTER

How do I know?
Because my name
is right here. B-L-U-E.
Blue!

Meet My Family

by Deborah Reber
illustrated by Victoria Miller

Hi! We are taking a family  today. Do
you know everyone?
Come with me!

PICTURE

81

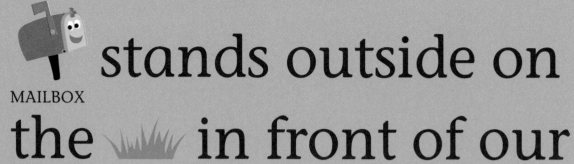 stands outside on

the  in front of our

He is and ⬛.
PURPLE   PINK
Sometimes 📫 has
MAILBOX
✉️ for me!
LETTERS

83

 is inside our

SIDETABLE DRAWER

HOUSE

in the living room.

She is .

RED

84

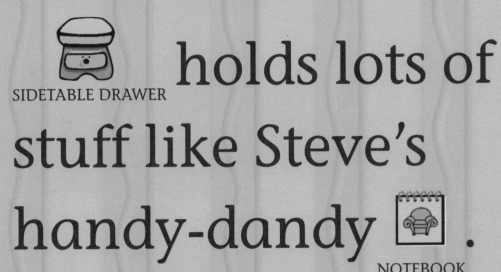 **SIDETABLE DRAWER** holds lots of stuff like Steve's handy-dandy  . **NOTEBOOK**

 and love to bake in the kitchen.

MR. SALT

MRS. PEPPER

BREAD

They help pack my  before I go to
LUNCHBOX

SCHOOL

in the morning.

 **and**  **take**

MR. SALT   MRS. PEPPER

care of  **. They**

PAPRIKA

really love her.

They like reading  BOOKS

to PAPRIKA before she

goes to sleep.

 and  live in the backyard.  is

SHOVEL   PAIL

SHOVEL

and  is .

YELLOW   PAIL   RED

I like to pick  with

FLOWERS

them. They love to

make .

SAND CASTLES

 lives in my bedroom. She sits on the  **TABLE** next to my  **BED**.

TICKETY

When  is excited,
TICKETY
she rings her bells.

Turquoise is my pet . I got her for my birthday!

TURTLE

Turquoise lives in a glass 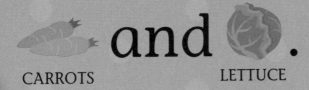 in my

BOWL

bedroom. She eats

 and .

CARROTS   LETTUCE

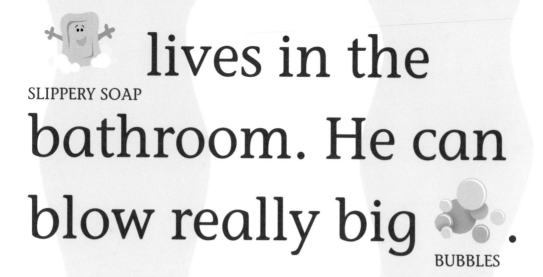

SLIPPERY SOAP lives in the bathroom. He can blow really big BUBBLES.

Together, we play in the  with our

and .

I love to play Blue's Clues with .

STEVE

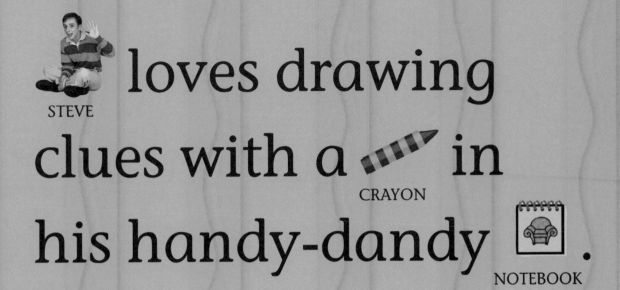 loves drawing

clues with a  in

his handy-dandy 🪑 .

STEVE

CRAYON

NOTEBOOK

Then there is me,  BLUE .
I love the color BLUE !

Oh! We need someone to take our family  ! Can you push the button?

PICTURE

Thank you!

My Pet Turtle

by Deborah Reber
illustrated by David Cutting

Hello! I am  BLUE.
Have you met my
pet TURTLE, Turquoise?

105

Turquoise was a birthday 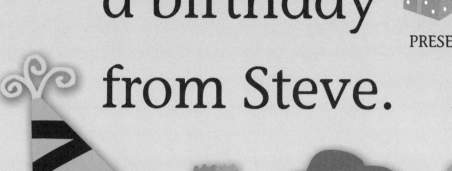 from Steve.

PRESENT

He gave me the  PRESENT
after I blew out the
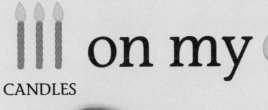 on my .

CANDLES   CAKE

107

Inside the 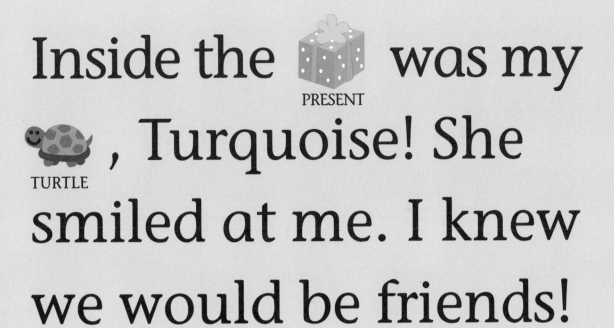 was my

TURTLE , Turquoise! She

smiled at me. I knew

we would be friends!

My , Turquoise,
lives in my bedroom.

TURTLE

She stays on the  TABLE

next to my 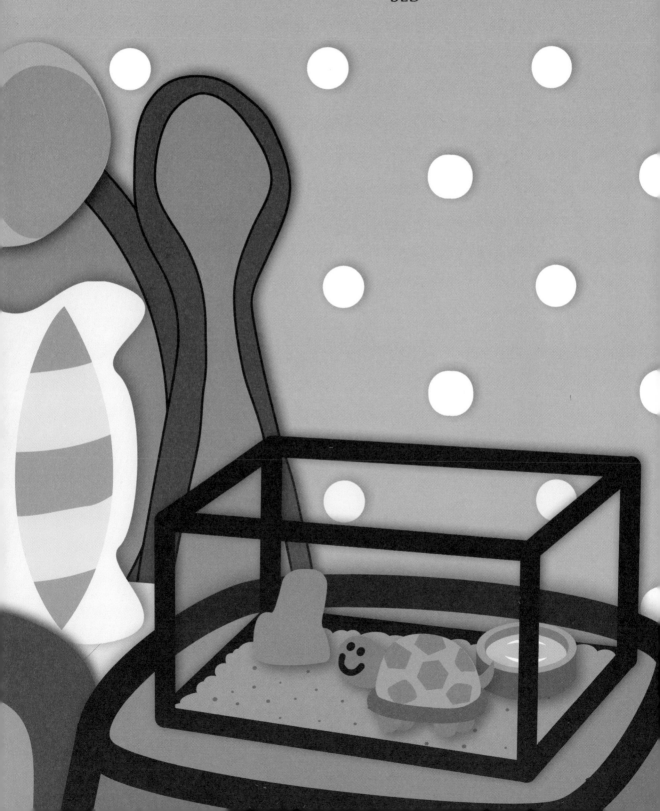 BED .

My  , Turquoise
lives in a glass .

TURTLE

TANK

She has sand and a rock in her .

TANK

I take care of my , TURTLE
Turquoise, by feeding
her every morning.

She likes to eat ,

CARROTS

, and .

LETTUCE   CELERY

My  TURTLE , Turquoise, needs WATER to drink.

116